The Strange Case of
Dr. Jekyll
and
Mr. Hyde

The Strange Case of Dr. Jekyll and Mr. Hyde

Adapted by Russell Punter

from the story by
Robert Louis Stevenson

Reading consultant: Alison Kelly

Series editor: Jane Chisholm

Cover and inside illustrations: Adrian Stone

First published in 2017 by Usborne Publishing Ltd.,
Usborne House, 83-85 Saffron Hill, London EC1N 8RT, England.
www.usborne.com

Contents

Chapter 1

Blackmail House

Mr. Utterson the lawyer was a very successful man. His business in the heart of London was a thriving one, due in no small part to his personality. Despite the fact that he could sometimes be unemotional and rather quiet, he was a likeable fellow. He would listen to people's troubles, rather than reprimand them.

This willingness to listen came easily to Mr. Utterson, as he felt it hard to express his own feelings openly. Even his friendships tended to be conducted in a serious way.

He lived alone, apart from his servants, and his only close friends were colleagues whom he'd known for a long time, or members of his own family. One such person was his distant cousin Mr. Richard Enfield, a well-known man about town. Enfield spent his evenings dining with the rich and famous of the city and had a reputation for enjoying the finer things in life.

To many it was a mystery what these two men could possibly have in common. People who saw them on their Sunday walks noticed that the pair said nothing, and looked so bored that they appeared relieved when they were approached by someone they knew. Despite this, the friends considered these walks the highlight of their week and set aside all their business so that they could enjoy them without interruption.

It so happened that one of these walks led them down a side street in a busy part of London. The street was small and narrow, and during the week would be packed with traders. On Sundays, however, it was quiet, and with its freshly painted shutters, well-polished door knockers and general cleanliness, it was a stylish sight.

Two doors down from one corner, however, there was a courtyard that sat below a rather sinister-looking building. It was two floors high, with just a single door at ground level. In contrast to the homes around it, it seemed to have been rather neglected. The black door, which had neither a bell nor a knocker, was blistered and faded. Beggars would often slouch against it and schoolboys had scratched the paintwork with their pocketknives. No one ever came out to drive these unwelcome visitors away, nor to repair the damage they caused.

One mild Sunday morning in spring 1883, Utterson and his friend were passing the courtyard when Enfield lifted up his walking cane and pointed.

"Did you ever notice that door?" he asked.

Utterson nodded.

"It's connected in my mind with a very odd story," said Enfield.

"Indeed," said his friend, with a note of interest in his voice, "and what was that?"

"Well," began Enfield, "about two months ago, I was returning home this way at about three o'clock one black morning. In street after street, everyone was asleep and I felt so alone that I began to long for the sight of a policeman. All at once, I saw two figures: one a little man, who was plodding along eastwards at a fast pace, and the other a girl of maybe eight or ten who was running as hard as she could down a cross street.

"Well sir, the two ran into one another at the corner. But then came the horrible part. For the man trampled calmly over the child's body and left her screaming on the ground.

"I say man, but he was more like some runaway train. I shouted at him to stop, then ran after the fellow and brought him back. He was perfectly calm and put up no resistance, but he gave me such an ugly look that it made me sweat with fear.

"By now there was quite a group gathered around the crying child, some of whom turned out to be her family. When the doctor who'd been sent for arrived, he declared that the girl was more frightened than injured. So there you might suppose would be an end to it. But there was something about the running man that made me want to punish him.

"I'd taken an instant dislike to him, as had the child's family, understandably. Every time the doctor looked at my prisoner, I saw him turn sickly white and a murderous look came into his eyes. I knew what was in the doctor's mind, just as he knew what was in mine. Killing this fiend being out of the question, we did the next best thing. We told him we would make a scandal out of this matter that would make his name stink from one end of London to the other. If he had any friends, we vowed that he would lose them. All the while we were telling him this, we were trying to keep a circle of angry women away from him, for they were as wild as harpies.

"Meanwhile, the man had a kind of black, sneering coolness about him. However, I also sensed a look of fear in his eyes, though he managed to hide it in his voice.

"'If you choose to make something out of this accident, I'm helpless to stop you,' he said. 'As a gentleman, I wish to avoid a scene, so name your price.'

"Well, we made him agree to pay a hundred pounds to the child's family. So the next thing to do was to get the money. And where do you think he led us, but to this very door?

"He whipped out a key, went in and came back a few moments later with ten pounds in gold and a cheque for the remainder. The cheque was from the bank account of a well-known gentleman whose name I won't repeat. Naturally I told the rogue that the whole business looked suspicious. People don't walk through a back door at three in the morning and come out with another man's cheque for nearly a hundred pounds.

"But he was quite calm. 'Set your mind at rest,' he sneered. 'I will stay with you until the banks open and cash the cheque myself.'

"So the man, the doctor, the child's father and I set off and spent the rest of the night at my office.

"First thing the next morning, we went to the bank. I gave in the cheque myself and said that I had every reason to believe that it was a forgery. But not a bit of it. It turned out to be genuine."

"Dear me," said Utterson sadly.

"I can see you feel the same way I do," said Enfield. "For the man I'd caught was a really evil character, yet the fellow who had written the cheque is a most respectable gentleman, famous for his charity work. I suppose he must be being blackmailed by this villain, probably for some embarrassing incident when he was a young man. 'Blackmail House' is what I call that place with the door as a result."

"Do you know if the man who wrote the cheque lives here?" asked Utterson.

"That would make sense, wouldn't it?" replied his friend. "But I happened to catch a brief glimpse of his address on the paperwork at the bank. He lives in some square or other."

"So you didn't find out his exact address, in order to ask him about the place with the black door?" asked Utterson.

"No sir," replied Enfield. "I make it a rule never to ask questions that might lead to awkward situations for all concerned."

"A very good rule, too," said Utterson.

"But I've studied this place," continued Enfield, gesturing at the courtyard. "It seems scarcely a house. There's no other door, and nobody goes in or out of it, apart from that wicked man, and then only rarely. There are three windows looking out onto the court on the first floor; none below. The windows are always shut, but they're clean. There is a chimney that is usually smoking, so somebody must live there; although it's hard to say for sure, as the buildings here are so packed together it's difficult to tell where one ends and another begins."

"While I agree with your rule about not asking questions," began Utterson, "do you know the name of the man who walked over the child?"

"Well," replied Enfield, "I can't see what harm it would do to tell you. It was a man named Hyde."

"Hm," said Utterson. "What did he look like?"

"He's not easy to describe," said Enfield. "There's something wrong with his appearance; something displeasing, something downright detestable. I never saw a man I so disliked, and yet I don't really know why. He had something deformed about him, although I can't say what exactly. He's an extraordinary-looking man, but I can't convey my impression of him in any real detail."

Utterson walked on for some time, deep in thought, before asking, "You're sure he had a key?"

"Why do you ask?" said his friend in surprise.

"The fact is," said Utterson, "the reason I haven't asked you the name of the man who wrote the cheque is because I already know it. I'm familiar with the owner of the house."

"I think you might have said so earlier," said Enfield, somewhat hurt. "But I've been exact. Hyde had a key, and what's more, he still has it. I saw him use it, not a week ago."

Mr. Utterson sighed deeply but said nothing.

"This is another lesson not to talk about things like this," said Enfield. "I'm ashamed of my loose tongue. Let's promise never to refer to this matter again."

"Agreed," said Utterson, "with all my heart."

Chapter 2

The Will

That evening, Utterson returned home in a sad mood and sat down to dinner without any real enthusiasm. After his Sunday evening meal, he usually sat by the fire and read until the clock of the nearby church chimed twelve, after which he would retire to bed. On this night, however, as soon as he left the dinner table he took a candle and went into his study. There he opened his safe and took out a document with the words 'The Last Will and Testament of Dr. Henry Jekyll' written on the front. With a serious expression on his face, he sat down to study the contents. Although Utterson had agreed to take charge of the Will, he had refused to assist in the making of it in any way.

The document stated that 'in the event of the death of Henry Jekyll, M.D., all his possessions are to pass into the hands of his friend and benefactor Edward Hyde'.

It went on to say that in the case of Dr. Jekyll's 'disappearance or unexplained absence for any period exceeding three calendar months', Edward Hyde would inherit everything that Dr. Jekyll possessed, aside from the payment of a few small sums to certain members of the doctor's household.

For a long time, this document had offended Utterson, both as a lawyer and as a rational man. It had been bad enough when Hyde was a stranger to him. Now he knew the man to be so detestable, it was even worse.

"Before, I thought this Will was merely mad," he said to himself as he replaced the offensive document in his safe. "Now I'm beginning to feel it's a disgrace."

With that, he blew out the candle, put on his coat and set off in the direction of Cavendish Square where his friend the great Dr. Lanyon lived and worked. "If anyone knows about this Hyde, it will be Lanyon," he thought.

A short while later, Dr. Lanyon's butler ushered Utterson straight into the dining room, where his master sat sipping a glass of wine. Lanyon was a hearty, healthy, red-faced gentleman with a shock of prematurely white hair.

At the sight of Utterson, he sprang out of his chair and welcomed the lawyer rather theatrically with both hands. The two had been friends since their schooldays. They respected each other and thoroughly enjoyed one another's company.

After some trivial chatter, Utterson broached the subject that had brought him there that night.

"I suppose," he said, "that you and I must be

Henry Jekyll's oldest friends?"

"I wish we were *younger* friends," chuckled Lanyon. "But I suppose we are. Though what difference does it make? I hardly see him now."

"Really?" said Utterson, "I'm surprised to hear you say that. I thought the two of you had so much in common."

"We *had*," replied Lanyon with a snort. "But it's more than ten years since Henry Jekyll became too eccentric for me. He began to lose his mind. I continue to take an interest in him for old times' sake, but I very rarely see him these days."

The doctor's face suddenly flushed purple.

"The kind of unscientific balderdash he started to come out with would have enraged the greatest medical men in history!"

This little fit of temper came as a relief to Utterson. "So they've only argued over some scientific point," he thought to himself. "It's nothing worse than that."

He gave Lanyon time to recover his composure

before asking the question he'd come to put.

"Have you ever come across a follower of his," he asked, "one Edward Hyde?"

"Hyde?" repeated Lanyon. "No, never heard of him. He must be after my time."

Having gathered this small amount of information, Utterson wished Lanyon goodnight and trudged back to his lonely house.

Chapter 3

Hyde and seek

Utterson tossed and turned in bed all night, his mind still full of unanswered questions.

As the bells of the church struck six o'clock, he was still running over the problem. Up until now, it had only been a dilemma based on cold facts. But now his imagination had taken over. As he lay awake in the darkness, Enfield's tale swam before his eyes. He could see the rows of glaring lamps stretching across the sleeping city, then the figure of a man walking swiftly, the child running from the other direction, then the collision as the human steam train trod the child underfoot and passed on, regardless of her screams.

Or else he would see a room in a rich house, where his friend Jekyll lay contentedly asleep. Then the door of that room would be opened and the curtains around the bed pulled apart. There stood a man who commanded Jekyll to follow him. Jekyll had no choice but to rise from his bed and obey.

Even if Utterson dozed off, he could see that sinister figure gliding stealthily through sleeping households and the labyrinths of the lamplit city. At every street corner the monster crushed a child and left her screaming.

And yet this figure had a face that melted before his eyes before he could make it out. So Utterson grew more and more determined to see the features of the real Mr. Hyde. If he could just once set eyes on him, then perhaps the mystery would be partly, even if not completely, resolved. He might discover a reason for Jekyll's strange desire to be associated with this man and for the peculiar clauses of the Will.

"If he's Mr. Hyde," he said to himself, "then I shall be Mr. Seek."

From that day forward, Utterson began to haunt the door in that side street.

In the morning, before office hours, at noon when the shops were busy and bustling with customers, at night under the fog-covered city moon, at all hours of the day or night, Utterson could be found at his lookout post.

Then at last his patience was rewarded.

It was a fine, dry night with frost in the air. The lamps, unshaken by any wind, threw a steady pattern of light and shadow on the street below.

By ten o'clock, the shops were closed. The side street stood deserted and, apart from the low rumblings of London all around, it was quite silent.

Mr. Utterson had been standing at his vantage point for a few minutes when he became aware of odd, light footsteps coming nearer. In the course of his nightly patrols, he'd grown used to the way the sound of footsteps suddenly came out of the darkness, even thought their owner might be some distance away. Yet he'd never felt more apprehensive than he did at that moment. It was with a strong sense of anticipation that he slunk back into the shadows of the courtyard.

The footsteps drew quickly nearer, becoming louder as they turned into the street. Utterson peered out from his hiding place to see just what kind of man he was dealing with.

The figure was small and very plainly dressed. Even at this distance, there was something about the furtive way he moved that Utterson found disturbing. The man made straight for the door and drew a key from his pocket.

Utterson stepped out and tapped the man on the shoulder. "Mr. Hyde, I think?"

Hyde shrank back with a hissing intake of breath. But his lack of composure only lasted a moment.

Without looking Utterson in the face, he answered coolly, "That's my name. What do you want?"

"I see you're going inside," said the lawyer. "I'm an old friend of Dr. Jekyll's – Mr. Utterson, you must have heard my name? Meeting you here so conveniently, I thought you might let me in."

"Dr. Jekyll's not at home," replied Hyde, putting the key in the lock. "How did you know who I was?" he added, still without looking up.

"Will you do something for me?" asked Utterson, ignoring Hyde's question.

"Certainly," replied Hyde. "What shall it be?"

"Will you let me see your face?" asked the lawyer.

Hyde hesitated for a moment as if considering the request. Then, with an air of defiance, he spun around. The pair stared at each other for a few seconds.

"Now I shall know you again," said Utterson.

"It might turn out to be useful."

"Yes, it's a good thing that we've met," replied Hyde. "I must let you have my address," he added, before giving the number of a street in Soho.

"The fellow suddenly seems very forthcoming," thought Utterson, suspiciously. His mind turned to the dreaded Will. "Perhaps he wants to make sure I know where he lives, so he can be contacted if anything happens to Jekyll?"

"And now," said Hyde, returning to his earlier question, "how did you know who I was?"

"By description," replied Utterson.

"Whose description?"

"We have friends in common," said Utterson.

"Common friends?" echoed Hyde hoarsely. "Who are they?"

"Jekyll, for instance," said Utterson.

"He never told you," cried Hyde, his face flushing red with anger. "I didn't expect you to lie to me, sir!"

"Come," said Utterson, "that's rather insulting."

Hyde snarled a savage laugh, and with extraordinary speed, unlocked the door and disappeared into the house.

Chapter 4

The house guest

Utterson stood uneasily in the courtyard for a moment. Then he walked back along the street, a puzzled expression on his face. He felt oddly disturbed by his encounter and tried to pinpoint the reason by going over in his mind what he'd learned.

Mr. Hyde was pale and short and gave the impression of being somehow deformed, though without actually showing any physical signs of this. He had an evil smile and had behaved towards Utterson with an unsettling mixture of timidity and boldness. He was capable of sharp rudeness and spoke with a husky, whispering, broken voice. All these were points against him, it was true. Yet none of them could completely explain the sensation of disgust, loathing and fear that Utterson felt towards the man.

"There must be something else," thought the lawyer. "If only I could find a name for it. Good heavens, the man seems so brutish. Or rather like some sort of caveman. Poor Jekyll. If ever a man had the face of the Devil, it's your new friend Hyde."

Around the corner from the side street, there was a row of old, grand houses. These houses backed onto the side street and as such, the little doors in the side street formed rear entrances to the grand houses. If Enfield had bothered to take more notice of the paperwork he'd seen at the bank, he would have realized that the address mentioned was one of these grand houses. At the front door of the house in question, Mr. Utterson now stopped and knocked. A small, thin, well-dressed servant opened the door.

"Is Dr. Jekyll at home, Poole?" asked Utterson.

"I will see, Mr. Utterson, sir," replied the butler, showing the lawyer inside. After a while, he returned to announce that Dr. Jekyll had gone out.

"I saw Mr. Hyde go in by the laboratory door," said Utterson. "Is that alright, when the doctor is away from home?"

"Quite alright, Mr. Utterson," replied Poole. "Mr. Hyde has a key."

"Your master seems to have placed a good deal of trust in that young man," said Utterson thoughtfully.

"Yes, indeed," said Poole. "We all have orders to obey him."

"I don't think I've ever met Mr. Hyde here?" said Utterson.

"Oh dear no, sir. He never dines here," replied the butler. "We see very little of him on this side of the house. He mostly comes and goes by the laboratory, you see."

Utterson wished Poole good night and set off for home with a heavy heart.

"Poor Jekyll," he thought to himself. "I'm sure he's in trouble. Perhaps Hyde has discovered some dark secret from Jekyll's past and is threatening to use it against him unless he agrees to his demands? Whatever the reason, surely Jekyll can't have agreed to be so generous to Hyde voluntarily?"

The idea suddenly gave Utterson a spark of hope.

"This Hyde must have secrets of his own; dark secrets by the look of him, secrets that would make those of Jekyll look like nothing. Things can't continue like this, that's for sure. It makes my blood run cold to think of a creature like Hyde under Jekyll's roof. And if he knows about the contents of the Will, he may become impatient to inherit. I must do something about the situation – if only Jekyll will let me."

A fortnight later, Utterson found himself a guest at one of Jekyll's dinner parties. After the other guests had departed, the lawyer remained behind to chat. This was nothing unusual, as Jekyll enjoyed Utterson's company and tonight was no exception.

Henry Jekyll was a tall, handsome, smooth-faced man of fifty, with a rather roguish yet kindly look about him. As he sat on the opposite side of the fireplace to his old friend, it was clear from his expression that he had a sincere and warm affection for him. This gave Utterson the confidence to bring up a subject he knew might be sensitive.

"I've been wanting to speak to you about that Will of yours," he began.

A close observer might have spotted a slight trace of annoyance on Jekyll's face. But he managed to hide it with the lightheartedness of his reply.

"My poor Utterson," he said, "I never saw anyone so distressed by anything as you were by my Will. Except, perhaps, for that old-fashioned fool Lanyon with regard to my scientific ideas. I tell you, I've never been more disappointed in any man than I am in Lanyon."

"You know I never approved of that Will," said Utterson, ignoring Jekyll's change of subject.

"I know, very well," said the doctor a little sharply. "You've told me so."

"Well, I'm telling you again," continued Utterson. "I've been learning things about young Hyde."

Jekyll's face turned pale and his eyes seemed to grow darker. "I don't want to hear any more about it," he said. "I thought we'd agreed to let this matter drop."

"What I heard was abominable," said Utterson.

"It won't change things. You don't understand the position I'm in," said Jekyll vaguely. "My situation is very strange. It's one of those things that can't be fixed by talking about it."

"You know you can trust me, Jekyll," said the lawyer. "Tell me all about it and I'm sure I can help you."

"My dear Utterson," said Jekyll, "this is very good of you. I can't thank you enough and I trust you more than any man alive. But it's not what you think. It's not as bad as that. Just to put your mind at rest, I'll tell you one thing. The moment I choose, I can be rid of Mr. Hyde, I give you my word. But this is a private matter and I beg you to say no more about it."

Utterson sat looking into the fire thoughtfully.

"No doubt you're right," he said at last, getting to his feet.

"Well, since we've brought up the matter for the last time," said Jekyll, "there is one point I'd like you to understand. I have a very great interest in poor Hyde. I know you've seen him, because he told me, and I'm afraid he may have been rude to you. But if I'm no longer around, I want you to promise me that you'll take care of Hyde and make sure he receives everything he's entitled to. I feel certain that you'd do that for me if you knew everything there is to know about the matter. So it would be a weight off my mind if you'd make that promise."

"I can't pretend that I'll ever like him," said Utterson.

"I don't ask that," pleaded Jekyll, laying his hand on his friend's arm. "I only ask you to help him for my sake, when I'm gone."

Utterson heaved a long sigh. "I promise."

Chapter 5

Murder

Nearly a year later, London was shocked by a violent and startling crime, made even more notable due to the identity of the victim.

A maid was alone one night in a house not far from the river. She had gone upstairs to bed at about eleven o'clock, and happened to be looking out of her window, when she witnessed a most terrible incident.

The night was cloudless and the lane, which was overlooked by the maid's room, was brilliantly lit by the full moon. As she sat looking out, the maid saw a well-dressed, elderly, white-haired gentleman walking up the lane, while a very short man approached from the opposite end. When they got within speaking distance of each other, the old gentleman bowed and began talking to the other in what appeared to be a friendly manner. From the old man's gestures it seemed to the maid that he was asking for directions. It was then that she first noticed the face of the other man, and recognized him as a certain Mr. Hyde, who had once visited her master and to whom she'd taken an instant dislike. This Hyde was carrying a heavy cane which he was slapping firmly into his palm while listening with obvious impatience to the other man.

Then all of a sudden, Hyde erupted into a great rage, stamping his foot and waving the cane in the air. The old gentleman took a step backwards in surprise, at which point Hyde clubbed him down. The next moment, Hyde trampled his victim under foot with an ape-like fury. He then rained down a series of blows which the maid could hear shattering the old gentleman's bones. Shocked by the horror of these sights and sounds, she fell into a dead faint.

It was two o'clock when she came around and called for the police. The murderer had long gone, but there lay his victim in the middle of the lane, fatally injured.

Although the stick which had done the deed was of some rare and very hard wood, it had broken in the middle under the stress of the attack. One splintered half had rolled into the gutter while the other had presumably been carried off by the murderer.

A wallet and a gold watch were found on the victim, but no cards or papers, except a sealed, stamped envelope which the gentleman had probably been carrying to post, and which bore the name and address of Mr. Utterson.

Later that morning, the police took the envelope to Utterson's house. When he'd been told what had occurred, he looked solemn. "I shall say nothing until I've seen the body," he said.

He was taken to the police station where the officer in charge of the case, Inspector Newcomen, showed him the body of the dead man.

"Yes," said Utterson, "I recognize him. He was a client of mine. I'm sorry to say that this is Sir Danvers Carew."

"Good grief, sir," exclaimed the officer, "is it possible?" His eyes lit up with ambition. Sir Danvers Carew was a renowned and much respected member of parliament. "This will be an infamous crime," said the inspector. "Perhaps you can lead us to the culprit, sir?" He briefly told Utterson what the maid had witnessed and let him see the broken cane.

Utterson had already been shaken by the mention of Hyde's name. But when what was left of the stick was laid before him, despite its condition, he recognized it at once as one he had given to Henry Jekyll as a gift many years before.

Utterson wanted to be totally assured about the

identity of Carew's attacker before he made his next move. "Is this Mr. Hyde a *small* man?" he asked.

"Particularly small and particularly wicked-looking, according to the maid," replied the officer.

That settled it. "If you will come with me in a cab," said Utterson, "I think I can take you to his house."

By this time it was about nine in the morning, and a dark brown fog lowered over the skies. As the cab neared its destination, that dismal quarter of Soho, with its muddy ways and slovenly inhabitants, looked to Utterson like somewhere in a nightmare.

The cab drew up in front of the address which Hyde had given to Utterson on the night they met. At that moment, the fog lifted and revealed the dingy street in all its foul glory. There was a low drinking house at one end and a shop selling twopenny salads at the other, while ragged children huddled in doorways. This was the home of Henry Jekyll's chosen heir to a quarter of a million pounds.

A pale, silver-haired old woman opened the door.

She had an evil expression about her, that looked as if it was well-used to deception. But her manners were excellent. Yes, she said, this was Mr. Hyde's residence, but he was not at home. He had been in that night very late, but had gone straight out again less than an hour later. There was nothing strange in that, she added: his habits were very irregular and he was often away. For instance, until yesterday it had been nearly two months since she'd last set eyes on him.

"We wish to see his rooms," said Utterson firmly.

At first, the woman declared that this was impossible.

Utterson gestured to the man by his side. "I'd better tell you that this is Inspector Newcomen of Scotland Yard."

A flash of ghoulish joy appeared on the woman's pasty face. "Ah!" she said. "He is in trouble. What has he done?"

Utterson and the inspector exchanged glances. "He doesn't seem a very popular character," said the officer quietly to the lawyer. "And now, my good woman," he said, turning back to the housekeeper, "just let me and this gentleman have a look around."

Apart from the old woman, Hyde was the only resident of the house. He had only used a couple of rooms, but they were nevertheless furnished in luxurious good taste. There was a cupboard filled with wine along with silver cutlery and delicate linen. A fine oil painting hung on the wall, which Utterson supposed must be a gift from Jekyll, who was a knowledgeable art collector.

At that moment, however, it was clear that the rooms had been recently ransacked; clothes lay strewn about the floor, with their pockets turned out. Drawers hung open, and on the hearth of the fireplace was a pile of ashes, as though many papers had been burned. From the embers the inspector unearthed the stub end of a green cheque book. A further search of the room uncovered the missing half of the walking stick. As this confirmed the inspector's suspicions, he was quite delighted.

Following up the clue of the cheque book, the two men then visited the bank it came from and discovered that Hyde's account contained several thousand pounds.

"I've got him now, sir," the inspector told Utterson as they left the bank. "He must have panicked, otherwise he'd never have left the walking stick behind and burned the cheque book. All we have to do now is wait for him to visit the bank to draw out his money. In the meantime, I'll get handbills circulated asking for information on his whereabouts."

Sadly for the inspector, such information was not forthcoming. My Hyde had few acquaintances – the maid's master had only seen him once, regarding some scientific matter. Hyde's family couldn't be traced, and the few people who could describe him all gave wildly different descriptions. These people only agreed about one thing – there was something about Hyde that was hauntingly inhuman.

Chapter 6

A mysterious letter

It was late in the afternoon when Mr. Utterson paid a call on Dr. Jekyll. He was shown in by Poole who took him through the house and out across a courtyard until they came to the building known as the laboratory. Although he knew about this part of the house, this was the first time that Utterson had actually been inside. He eyed the dingy windowless room with curiosity. The tables were laden with chemical apparatus, in keeping with the doctor's profession, while the floor was strewn with crates and littered with packing straw.

At the far end, a flight of steps led up to a red baize door. Poole opened this door onto what was evidently the doctor's study. It was a large room, with three dusty windows barred with iron which looked out upon the courtyard. A fire burned in the grate, a lamp was lit above the chimney and there, huddled by the fire, sat Dr. Jekyll, looking deadly sick. He didn't get up, but greeted Utterson in a quiet voice and held out a hand.

Utterson shook it. It was icy to the touch. "You've heard the news?" the lawyer asked, as soon as Poole had left them.

Jekyll shuddered. "The newspaper sellers were crying it in the square," he said. "I heard them in my dining room."

"Carew was my client, but so are you," said Utterson, his voice filled with concern. "Please tell me you haven't been foolish enough to hide his murderer?"

"I swear I'll never set eyes on him again," cried Jekyll. "I give you my word I'm done with him. It's all at an end. Indeed, he doesn't want my help. Mark my words, he will never be heard of again."

Utterson listened gloomily. "You seem pretty sure of him," he said. "I only hope for your sake that you're right. If it came to trial, your name might appear in the case."

"I have reasons to be certain, but I can't share them with anyone," replied Jekyll. "However, there is one thing on which I would like your advice."

He handed Utterson a folded sheet of paper. "I've received this letter, and I don't know if I should show it to the police. I trust your judgement on the matter."

The letter was written in odd, sloped handwriting and was signed 'Edward Hyde'. It stated that Dr. Jekyll should have no fears for his safety, as Hyde had a means of escape which was sure to succeed.

"Have you got the envelope?" asked Utterson.

"I burned it," replied Jekyll. "But it had no postmark, the letter was delivered by hand."

"I shall sleep on the matter," said Utterson. "Now answer me this: it was Hyde who dictated the terms of your Will, wasn't it?"

Jekyll nodded.

"I thought so," said Utterson. "You realize he meant to murder you? You've had a narrow escape."

"I've had something far more important," replied his friend solemnly. "I've had a lesson. Oh, what a lesson I've had." So saying, the doctor covered his face with his hands.

The mood had become too uncomfortable for Utterson to linger, so he said his goodbyes and saw himself out via the main house. On his way, he stopped to speak to the butler.

"By the way, Poole," he said, "there was a letter handed in today. What did the messenger look like?"

"No letters have been delivered by hand today sir," replied Poole.

So it was that Utterson walked home with his fears renewed. It seemed the letter must have been delivered by the laboratory door, possibly even to the doctor's study itself. In which case, it needed to be dealt with more cautiously. He felt in need of advice, and there was one person who might be able to give it.

There was no man from whom Utterson kept fewer secrets than his head clerk, Mr. Guest. He knew Dr. Jekyll and his household and could scarcely failed to have heard about Hyde's familiarity with the house. Wasn't it natural that Utterson should show his employee a letter that put that mystery to rights? Guest also happened to be an expert on handwriting. He was sure to have some opinion, and from that Utterson could decide on his own course of action.

He invited the clerk to dine with him, and as they sat by the fire afterwards, he introduced the subject of Sir Danvers' death.

"The murderer was deranged of course," sighed Guest.

"I should like your views on that," said Utterson,

handing him the letter given to him by Jekyll. "I have this document in Hyde's handwriting. I don't know what to do about it, but it's in your field of expertise."

Guest's eyes brightened and he studied the letter with passion.

"I've revised my first thought, sir," he said at last. "He's not deranged, but the handwriting *is* odd."

At that moment, a servant entered with a note for Utterson.

"Is that from Dr. Jekyll?" asked Guest. "I think I recognize the handwriting."

"It's just an invitation to dinner," replied his host. "Why? Do you want to see it?"

"One moment, thank you, sir," said Guest. He laid the two sheets of paper alongside each other and stared at them.

"Why do you compare them?" asked Utterson, intrigued.

"Well sir," replied Guest, "there's a rather singular resemblance. The two hands are in many ways identical, only one is strangely sloped."

"How odd," said Utterson. He paused. "I wouldn't speak to anyone about this note, Guest."

"No sir," said his clerk. "I understand."

When Guest had left, Utterson locked the note in his safe.

"Has Henry Jekyll forged a letter for a murderer?" he thought to himself.

His blood ran cold.

Chapter 7

Death of the doctor

Time passed. Thousands of pounds were offered as a reward for information leading to the arrest of Edward Hyde. But it seemed the man had disappeared so completely, it was if he had never existed. Much of his past was unearthed. Tales came out about his callous and violent cruelty, of his strange associates, of the hatred that seemed to have surrounded his deeds. But of his present whereabouts, not a whisper. From the time he left the house in Soho on the morning of the murder, Hyde simply vanished from the world.

As the weeks turned to months, Mr. Utterson began to recover from his initial feelings of distress and became more relaxed in his mind. The death of Sir Danvers had been tragic, but at least it had resulted in the disappearance of Mr. Hyde.

Now Hyde's evil influence was gone, a new life seemed to begin for Dr. Jekyll too. He came out of his seclusion and renewed his acquaintance with his old friends. His charity work took up much of his time. Overall, he appeared brighter and more cheerful, and for two months or so the doctor was at peace.

On the 8th of January, Utterson dined at Jekyll's, along with a small party of guests including Dr. Lanyon. On the face of it, their host looked just as he had when the trio had been inseparable friends.

But just a few days later, on the 12th, and again on the 14th, Utterson wasn't permitted to see Dr. Jekyll.

"Dr. Jekyll is confined to the house," Poole said solemnly. "He will see no one."

On the 15th, Utterson tried again, and was once more refused entry. Having been used to seeing his friend almost daily, this sudden change made Utterson feel anxious.

Two nights' later, he went to visit Dr. Lanyon. But when he entered his friend's drawing room, he was shocked at the change that had taken place in Lanyon's appearance. His rosy cheeks had grown pale, he had lost weight and he looked considerably older. Yet it was not so much these physical changes that struck Utterson, more the change in the doctor's personality. He seemed afraid. "Of impending death, perhaps?" thought Utterson. "Being a doctor, I suppose he would know if his days were numbered."

"I've had a shock," explained Lanyon, "and I'll never recover. It's a matter of weeks now. Well, life has been pleasant. I liked it. Or at least I used to like it."

"Jekyll is ill too," said Utterson. "Have you seen him?"

Lanyon's face changed, and he held up a trembling hand. "I wish to see or hear no more of Dr. Jekyll," he said in a loud, unsteady voice. "I'm quite finished with that person. Please don't mention his name, for I regard him as dead."

Utterson was shocked at the doctor's attitude. The pair's relationship had obviously deteriorated once again. But perhaps Lanyon could offer some advice. "Can I do anything to help him?" he asked.

"Nothing can be done," replied Lanyon. "Ask him yourself."

"He will not see me," said the lawyer.

"I'm not surprised," said Lanyon. "One day, after I'm dead, you might discover the facts of the matter, but I'm not able to tell you now. In the meantime, if you haven't anything else to discuss, then please go, for I cannot bear it."

As soon as he got home, Utterson wrote to Jekyll complaining about his exclusion from his house and asking about the cause of his broken friendship with Dr. Lanyon.

The next day brought a long reply. It seemed the quarrel with Lanyon could not be mended.

"I don't blame our old friend," wrote Jekyll, "but I share his view that we must never meet. From now on, I plan to lead a solitary life. You must not be surprised, nor doubt our friendship if my door is shut to you. You must let me go on my own dark way. I've brought a danger on myself that I can't discuss. It's my own fault and so I must suffer. I only ask that you respect my silence."

Utterson was amazed. What had caused all this? The dark influence of Hyde had gone. Jekyll had seemingly returned to his old, contented self. A week ago the future looked bright. Now, in a moment, friendship and peace of mind had been shattered. It seemed to have affected Jekyll so suddenly that Utterson would normally have put it down to some sickness. But there was something about what Lanyon had said that made him feel there was more to it than that.

A week later, Dr. Lanyon took to his bed. Less than a fortnight after that he was dead.

After the funeral, Utterson retreated to his study and placed an envelope on his desk, addressed in the handwriting of his late friend:

'PRIVATE: for the hands of J. G. Utterson ALONE, and if he should die before me, *to be destroyed unread.*'

Utterson dreaded what it might contain. "I've buried one friend today," he thought. "What if the contents of this packet cost me another?" He tore open the envelope. Inside was a second one, this time marked:

'Not to be opened until the death or disappearance of Dr. Henry Jekyll.'

Utterson couldn't believe his eyes. Here was that word again, 'disappearance', used in connection with Jekyll, just as it had been in that dreadful Will that he'd long since returned to his old friend.

But on that occasion the word had been dictated by the evil Hyde. Now it had been written by Dr. Lanyon. What could it mean?

For a moment Utterson was tempted to ignore the instruction on the second envelope and to read its contents. But loyalty to his late friend prevented him.

However, it was one thing for Utterson to curb his curiosity, quite another to eliminate it completely.

Chapter 8

A visit to Dr. Jekyll's

From the day of Lanyon's funeral, Utterson no longer desired the company of his friend Jekyll with the same eagerness he'd felt before. He thought of him kindly, but also with discomfort and dismay.

When he did call on Jekyll, he had to confess to a certain relief when he was once again refused admission. Utterson preferred to speak with Poole on the doorstep, in sight of the freedom of the city, than within the confines of Jekyll's sad house.

Poole told him that the doctor kept mostly to the

study over the laboratory, where he often spent the night. He said his master was sad and silent, as if there was something preying on his mind.

The butler told Utterson exactly the same thing every time he went to the house, and so the lawyer's visits became fewer and fewer.

It so happened that one Sunday, when Utterson was out on his weekly walk with Mr. Enfield, they found themselves strolling once again down the side street with the infamous door.

"Well," said Enfield, "that story's at an end, at least. We shall see no more of Mr. Hyde."

"I hope not," said Utterson. "Did I tell you that I met him once? I felt that same revulsion that you described."

"It was impossible not to," said Enfield. "By the way, what an idiot you must have thought me, not to have realized that this was a back way to Dr. Jekyll's. I only found out later."

"In that case," said Utterson, "let's step into the courtyard to take a look up at the windows of the doctor's study. To tell you the truth, I'm worried about poor Jekyll, and the presence of a friend, even outside, might do him good."

When the pair reached the courtyard they could see that the middle one of the three study windows was half open. Sitting close beside it, with the look of a helpless prisoner, was Dr. Jekyll.

"Hello! Jekyll!" cried Utterson. "Are you better?"

"I'm very low, Utterson," replied Jekyll wearily, "very low. It won't last long, thank goodness."

"You stay indoors too much," said Utterson. "You should be out and about like my cousin Mr. Enfield and me. Come now, get your hat and coat and take a quick walk with us."

"You're very kind," sighed Jekyll. "I should like to very much, but no, no, no, it's quite impossible. I dare not. But I'm very glad to see you. It's really a great pleasure. I would ask you and Mr. Enfield up, but the place isn't fit for visitors."

"Why then," said Utterson, "the best thing we can do is to speak with you from where we are."

"That's just what I was going to suggest," said Jekyll with a smile. But hardly had the words left his lips, when the smile vanished from his face, to be replaced by such a look of terror and despair that it froze the blood of the two gentlemen below. They only saw this expression for an instant, as the window was quickly slammed shut. That glimpse had been enough however, and they left the courtyard without exchanging a word.

It wasn't until they were some distance from the side street that Mr. Utterson at last turned and looked at his companion. They were both pale, with a look of horror still in their eyes.

Utterson felt a terrible guilt at fleeing from his old friend. But, under the circumstances, there was nothing more he could do. He was certain an attempt to gain entry at the front of the house would be met with the usual refusal. Enfield was aware of this too, but the same look of shame was on his face.

"May we be forgiven," said Utterson.

Enfield could only nod his head in agreement before walking on in silence.

Chapter 9

Disappearance

Several weeks later, Mr. Utterson was sitting by his fireside after dinner one wild, cold night when he was surprised to receive a visit from Poole.

"Bless me, Poole, what brings you here?" he cried. Noting the man's anxious expression, he added "What's the matter with you? Is the doctor ill?"

"Mr. Utterson," replied Poole. "There's something dreadfully wrong."

"Sit down and drink this glass of wine," said

Utterson. "Now take your time and tell me plainly what you want."

"The doctor's shut up in his study, as I told you before. But there's something funny going on in there. I don't like it, sir. Strike me dead if I like it. I'm afraid, Mr. Utterson."

"Be specific, Poole," said Utterson. "What exactly are you afraid of?"

"I've been in a state of fear for about a week," said Poole, ignoring the lawyer's question. "I can't bear it any more."

Poole certainly seemed scared. He'd hardly looked Utterson in the face, staring instead at a corner of the floor. Even the glass of wine in his hand went untasted.

"I can see there's something seriously amiss," said Utterson. "Try to tell me what it is."

"I think there's been foul play," whispered Poole.

"Foul play?" cried Utterson. "Whatever do you mean?"

"I daren't say, sir," replied Poole. "But will you

come along with me and see for yourself?"

Mr. Utterson rose to fetch his hat and coat, noticing the relief on Poole's face as he did so.

The cold streets of London were deserted as they made their way across town. Utterson wished it were otherwise. Never in his life had he longed more for the company of strangers. For in his heart he felt he was on his way to a tragedy.

When at last they reached Jekyll's house, Poole wiped his brow with his handkerchief. But his perspiration had been brought about not by exertion but by fear. For his face was white and his voice, when he spoke, was broken.

"Well, sir," he said, "here we are, and God grant there be nothing wrong."

He knocked on the door in a cautious manner. It opened a crack and a voice called out nervously,

"Is that you, Poole?"

"It's all right," replied Poole. "Open up."

Utterson entered the house to find every single servant huddled in the hall like a flock of sheep. At the sight of the lawyer, the cook ran forward, "Thank goodness, it's Mr. Utterson!" she cried.

"What are you all doing here in the hall?" asked Utterson, bemused.

"They're afraid," said Poole.

Then the housemaid broke into hysterical whimpering and had to be hushed by Poole.

"Now," said the butler, taking a candle from the pale-faced pantry boy, "if you'll just follow me, Mr. Utterson sir."

Poole led the lawyer through the house, across the garden and into the empty laboratory.

"I want you to hear him, sir," whispered Poole. "And if by any chance, he asks you to go in, don't."

When the pair reached the foot of the stairs, Poole motioned to Utterson to stand to one side. With an obvious attempt to steady his nerves, the butler climbed the steps and knocked somewhat nervously on the red baize door.

"Mr. Utterson is here, sir, asking to see you," he called, gesturing to Utterson to listen.

"Tell him I can't see anyone," came a voice from within.

"Thank you, sir," said Poole, with a note of satisfaction. He led Utterson quietly out of the laboratory, across the yard and into the kitchen of the main house.

"Sir," he said closing the door behind them, "was that *Dr. Jekyll's* voice you heard?"

"It certainly seems different," said Utterson.

"Different?" croaked the butler. "I should say so. I've worked here twenty years and I know my master's voice. No sir, the master's been murdered. He was murdered eight days ago, when I heard him cry out. So who's in there now, and why is he still there, that's what I want to know, Mr. Utterson!"

Chapter 10

Vengeance

"This is a very wild tale, my man," said Utterson. "Suppose it's as you say and Dr. Jekyll has been murdered. Why should the murderer stay behind? It doesn't make sense."

"Well, you're a hard man to convince sir," sighed Poole. "But I'll do it yet." He laid the candle down on the kitchen table and cleared his dry throat. "It was sometimes the master's way to write orders for things he wanted on scraps of paper and leave them out for us on the steps of the laboratory. Well every day this past week, sometimes twice a day, there have been orders from whoever's in that study to be taken to the wholesale chemist's in town. Every time I brought the stuff back, there would be another note telling me to return it, because it wasn't pure, together with another order to a different firm. I've heard him cry out in frustration for some sort of medicine. This drug is wanted badly, sir, whatever it's for."

"Do you still have any of these requests?" asked Utterson.

Poole felt in his pockets and produced a crumpled note. Utterson smoothed it out and held it up to the candlelight. It read:

'Dr. Jekyll presents his compliments to Messrs Maw. He assures them that their last sample is impure and quite useless for his present purpose. Some time ago, Dr. Jekyll purchased a somewhat large quantity from Messrs Maw. He now begs them to search most thoroughly, and should any of the same quality be left, to forward it to him at once. Expense is not a problem. The importance of this to Dr. Jekyll cannot be exaggerated.'

Thus far, the letter had been quite calm, but here the writing suddenly became less neat and the message more desperate:

'For pity's sake, find me some of the old substance.'

"This is a strange note," said Utterson. "Why do you still have it?"

"The man at Maw's threw it back at me in anger, sir," replied Poole.

"Do you recognize the handwriting?" asked Utterson.

"What does handwriting matter, sir?" said Poole somewhat impatiently. "I've *seen* the villain!"

"Seen him?" repeated Utterson. "When?"

"One day, I came into the laboratory from the garden," said Poole. "This imposter had slipped out of the study to look for this drug or whatever it is. There he was at the far end of the room, searching among the crates. He looked up when I came in and gave a cry, then dashed upstairs into the study. I only saw his face for a moment, but it made the hair upon my head stand up. Sir, if that was my master, why was he wearing a mask? If it was my master, why did he cry out like a rat, and run away?"

"These are very strange circumstances," interrupted Utterson. "But I think I have an explanation. Your master is obviously suffering from some medical condition which deforms the face. That would explain the mask, his wish not to be seen by his friends, and his desire to find a drug to effect a cure. It's sad, but natural enough. You've been worried unduly, I think."

"Sir," said the butler with an effort of self control, "that thing is not my master, and that's the truth. No sir, that thing in the mask was never Dr. Jekyll. Who knows what it was, but it was never Dr. Jekyll. I believe in my heart that he's been murdered."

"Poole," replied the lawyer, "if that's what you

truly believe, then it's my duty to make certain. Much as I want to spare the doctor's feelings, I now consider it my duty to break down the study door."

"Ah!" said Poole with a smile, "Now you're talking, Mr. Utterson. I shall help you do it."

"Well said," replied Utterson, "and whatever happens, I'll make sure you don't get into any trouble."

"There's a wood chopper in the laboratory," suggested Poole, "and you might bring the kitchen poker for yourself."

Utterson picked up the iron tool and weighed it in his hand. "You realize that you and I are about to place ourselves in some danger?" he said.

"Yes indeed, sir," replied the butler.

"In which case, I think we should be completely honest with each other. That masked man you saw. Did you recognize him?"

"Well, he moved so fast sir, and he was so doubled up, that I couldn't swear to that. But if you mean, was it Mr. Hyde? Why yes, I think it was! He was much the same height and moved in the same light-footed way. And who else could have gained entry through the laboratory door? You'll remember that at the time of the murder, he still had the key. But that's not all. I wonder, did you ever meet Mr. Hyde, sir?"

"Yes," replied Utterson. "I spoke to him once."

"Then you'll know that there was something odd about that gentleman. I don't rightly know how to describe it, other than to say he gave you a feeling that chilled your bones."

"I'll confess I felt something like that, yes," admitted the lawyer.

"Well, when that masked thing jumped like a monkey from among those crates and up into the study, a feeling shot down my spine like ice," said Poole. "Oh, I know it's not evidence, sir. But a man has his feelings, and I give you my word, it was Mr. Hyde!"

"Yes," said Utterson. "I'm beginning to think

you're right. I believe poor Jekyll has been killed
and that his murderer is still lurking in his victim's
room. Well, we shall avenge poor Henry. Brace
yourself, Poole. It's time we went on the offensive."

Chapter 11

Suicide

Poole summoned Bradshaw the footman and Utterson told him of their plan. He was instructed to arm himself and the pantry boy, and to take up a position at the laboratory door in the side street, in case their suspect attempted to escape that way. Utterson and Poole would give them ten minutes to reach their post.

Taking the poker under his arm, Utterson led Poole out across the yard. The clouds had thickened to cover the moon and it was now quite dark. The wind blew the light of the candle to and fro until they reached the shelter of the laboratory where they sat down silently to wait. Outside, London hummed solemnly, but in that room the quiet was broken only by the sound of footsteps pacing up and down in the study.

"That goes on night and day," whispered Poole. "It only stops for a while when a new sample comes from the chemist. And does that sound like the doctor's footsteps to you?"

Utterson had to admit it was different from the heavy creaking tread of Henry Jekyll. "Is there any other noise?" he asked.

Poole nodded. "Once, I heard him crying!"

"Crying?" said Utterson, suddenly feeling a chill of horror.

"Crying like a woman or a lost soul," added Poole. "I came away in such a state that I could have cried too."

The ten minutes drew to an end. Gripping the chopper in his hand, Poole joined Utterson as they moved towards the study door with bated breath.

"Jekyll!" cried Utterson loudly. "I demand to see you." He paused for a moment. There was no reply. "I give you fair warning, we are suspicious. I must and shall see you, if not by peaceful means, then by brute force!"

"Utterson," came a voice from beyond the door, "for pity's sake, have mercy!"

Utterson turned to Poole. "That's not Jekyll's voice," he cried, "it's Hyde's! Down with the door, Poole."

The butler swung the chopper with all his might. The blow shook the building, and the red baize door leaped against the lock and hinges. A dismal screech like a wounded animal rang from the study. Poole struck the door again, but the wood was tough and the fittings were well made. It was not until the fifth blow that the lock burst off and the remains of the door fell inwards onto the carpet.

Surprised for a moment by the silence that followed, Utterson and Poole stood back a little, then peered into the room. The fire glowed in the hearth, papers were laid out neatly on the desk and near the fire things were laid out for tea. It might have been said that it was the quietest, most ordinary room in London – except that in the middle of the study lay the bent up body of a man.

Utterson and Poole tiptoed up to it and turned it on its back. It was Edward Hyde. He was dressed in clothes far too large for him, more suited to Dr. Jekyll in fact. From the broken glass bottle in his hand and the strong smell of bitter almonds in the air, Utterson realized the man had poisoned himself with cyanide.

"We're too late either to save or to punish," he said sternly. "Hyde has gone to meet his maker. It only remains for us to find the body of your master."

They searched the study and the laboratory, but found no trace of Henry Jekyll. Then they went out into the corridor that led to the door in the side street. Poole stamped on the flagstones. "He must be buried under here," he said.

"Or he may have fled," said Utterson. He examined the door that led to the street. It was locked, and lying nearby on the ground they found the key, already stained with rust.

"Look, it's broken, sir," observed Poole, "as if someone had stamped on it."

"Yes," agreed Utterson, "and the cracks are rusty too." The two men exchanged looks. "This is beyond me, Poole," said the lawyer. "Let's go back to the study."

With an occasional glance at the body, the two men made a further examination of the room. On one table there were measured heaps of chemicals, as if an experiment had been in progress. "This is the same drug I was always bringing him," said Poole, pointing to one of the piles.

To one side of the room stood a simple full-length mirror.

"This must have seen some strange things," said Poole with a shiver.

"What did Jekyll..." Utterson corrected himself, "what *could* Jekyll possibly want with a mirror like this in here?"

"You might well ask, sir," replied Poole.

They turned their attention to the desk. On top of a neat pile of papers was a very large envelope addressed, in Jekyll's handwriting, to Utterson.

The lawyer opened it and three items fell out. One was Jekyll's Will, which was identical to the one Utterson had objected to, except for one thing. In place of the name Edward Hyde was that of John Gabriel Utterson. The lawyer looked at Poole, then back at the Will, then at the dead man on the carpet.

"I can't understand it," he said. "Hyde had the Will all this time. He must have been enraged to see that I'd replaced him. And yet he didn't destroy it."

He picked up the second document. It was a brief letter in Jekyll's handwriting. The first thing that Utterson noticed was that it was dated at the top – with that very day's date.

"Oh Poole," he cried hopefully, "Dr. Jekyll was alive and here today! He can't possibly have been murdered and disposed of in so short a time. He must still be alive and has fled. But why? And if so, can we be sure that Hyde's death was suicide? We must be careful. We may yet involve your master in some terrible crime."

"Why don't you read the letter, sir?" asked Poole.

"Because I'm worried," replied Utterson solemnly. "I only hope I have no need to be."

With that, he read the letter aloud:

My dear Utterson,

When this falls into your hands, I shall have disappeared. Under what circumstances, I cannot foresee, but my instinct tells me that the end is near at hand. Read the letter that Lanyon told me he had left for you after his death. Then, if you want to know more, read the accompanying confession of your worthy and unhappy friend,

HENRY JEKYLL

Utterson looked at the third item. It was a large packet, sealed in several places.

Utterson put it in his pocket and turned to Poole. "Say nothing about Dr. Jekyll's letter," he said. "If your master has fled or is dead, we may at least save his reputation. It's ten o'clock now. I must go home and read Dr. Lanyon's letter and the confession inside this package in quiet. But I'll be back before midnight, when we shall send for the police."

They went out, locking the laboratory door behind them.

Leaving Poole with the rest of the servants, Utterson walked briskly back to his office to read a letter and a confession which, in due course, would explain the whole mystery.

Chapter 12

Dr. Jekyll's secret

Utterson opened his safe and took out the letter that he'd kept there since Lanyon's death. With a sad sigh of expectation, he tore open the envelope and read the contents:

13th January 1885

Four days ago, I received by the evening post a registered letter from my colleague and old friend Henry Jekyll. I was surprised, as we weren't in the habit of writing to each other. I had dined with him the night before and I couldn't imagine he had

anything to tell me since then that would require
the security of a registered letter. It ran as follows:

Dear Lanyon,

You're one of my oldest friends and although
we've sometimes disagreed on matters of
science, I don't believe it has affected our
relationship. If you asked me to defend your
reputation, your sanity or your life, I would
sacrifce everything to help you. Lanyon, my
reputation, my sanity, my life are in your hands.
If you fail me tonight, I am lost. You might
be thinking that I'm going to ask you to do
something disreputable. Judge for yourself.

I want you to postpone whatever you had
planned for tonight, and to take this letter with
you to my house. You'll find Poole waiting for
you with a locksmith. Force him to open the door
to my study in the laboratory. Enter alone and
go to the large chest of drawers. Break the lock
if need be and take out the drawer marked 'E'. It
contains some powders, a small glass bottle and

a notebook. Carry the drawer and its contents back to your house exactly as you find it.

If you set out when you receive this letter, then you should be back before midnight. At that time, you must be alone in your consulting room. At twelve, a man will arrive who is aware of my name. Give him the drawer. By doing so, you will have earned my eternal gratitude. Five minutes later, you'll discover the reason behind what I've asked you to do. Then you'll realize just how much my sanity and my life depended upon it.

I can't bring myself to consider the possibility that you won't help me, but I'm sure that you will. Think of me as I write this, weighed down by the blackest depression you could imagine. Yet I know that, with your assistance, my troubles will be over.

Help me, my dear Lanyon, and save
your friend,
H.J.

Having read the letter, I was convinced my friend was insane. But Jekyll seemed so desperate I could hardly ignore his request. The only way to understand what the strange business was all about was to carry out the instructions.

I took a cab to Jekyll's house to find Poole waiting for me with a locksmith. Like myself, the loyal butler had received his instructions by registered letter. The three of us entered the laboratory and after some two hours' work the study door stood open. The chest of drawers was unlocked and so I took out the drawer marked 'E', wrapped it in a sheet and returned home.

The first thing I did was to examine the contents of the drawer in more detail. The powders were made up into packets, though it was clear that Jekyll had done so himself, as they weren't as neat as those dispensed by a high street chemist. When I opened one of the wrappers I found what seemed to be a simple, white, crystalline salt.

The glass bottle was half full of a blood-red liquid which smelled of phosphorus and ether, but I could make no guess at the other ingredients.

The notebook contained little but a series of dates covering a period of many years, though the entries stopped nearly a year ago. The occasional date was accompanied by a brief remark. 'Total failure!!!' was written alongside an early entry, and 'double' appeared half a dozen times.

All this was intriguing, but it didn't tell me anything definite. As far as I could see, it was just a bottle of chemicals, some salts and a record of experiments that didn't seem to have led anywhere, like so many of Jekyll's investigations. How could these things affect the reputation, the sanity or the life of my eccentric colleague? Why was it necessary for me to meet the man who was due to collect them in secret? The more I thought about it, the more convinced I became that I was dealing with a case of madness.

As I waited for Jekyll's mystery man to arrive, I loaded my old revolver just in case I should need to defend myself.

Twelve o'clock had barely rung out across London, when there was a light knock at the door. When I answered it, I found a small man leaning against the pillar of the porch.

"Have you come from Dr. Jekyll?" I asked.

He merely nodded. I gestured for him to enter and I couldn't help noticing that he glanced uneasily over his shoulder as he did so.

All of this made me somewhat nervous and I kept my hand on my revolver as I led him into the consulting room.

Here I was able to see him more clearly and I was struck by the shocking nature of his face. It seemed to throb with a muscular power that was at odds with the man's slight stature. He disturbed me greatly, but it wasn't just his appearance that caused this. It was something *much harder to explain. Thinking it over since then, I believe what I felt was an instinctive repulsion to something quite unnatural.*

This unsettling figure was dressed in a fashion that would have made any ordinary person look ridiculous. While his clothes were tasteful and expensive, they were far too large for him. His trousers sagged from his legs and were rolled up to keep them from dragging on the ground. The waist of the coat hung below his thighs and the collar sprawled wide across his shoulders. But far from making me laugh, this strange sight only made me more curious about the man's background.

From the moment he entered the room, my visitor was on fire with brooding excitement.

"Have you got it?" he cried, impatiently, grabbing me by the arm. "Have you got it?"

My blood froze at his wild action. "Come sir," I said, removing his hand, "Be seated, please."

"I beg your pardon, Dr. Lanyon," he replied

politely. "My impatience has made me forget my manners. I came here under instructions of your colleague, Dr. Henry Jekyll, on a matter of some urgency, and I understood..." he paused and put his hand to his throat. I could see that he was trying to remain calm. "I understood, a drawer..."

He was so distressed, I abandoned any idea of further conversation.

"There it is sir," I said, pointing to the drawer which lay on the floor behind the table and was covered once more by the sheet.

He sprang towards it, but paused and put his hand to his chest. I could hear his teeth grating and his face looked so ghastly that I was worried he was going to drop dead on the spot.

"Calm yourself," I said.

He looked at me with a dreadful smile and plucked off the sheet.

As soon as he saw the contents, he gave such a loud sob of relief that I sat petrified. When he spoke again it was in a much more controlled voice.

"Do you have a measuring glass?" he asked.

I went to a cupboard and gave him what he wanted. He thanked me with a smiling nod, measured out a small quantity of the red liquid and added one of the powders. At first the mixture retained its dark, reddish hue, but as the crystals dissolved, it became brighter and started to bubble, while at the same time giving off swirls of gas. Suddenly the bubbling stopped and the liquid changed to a dark purple which then faded to a watery green.

My visitor, who had been watching this metamorphosis keenly, smiled and put the glass down on the table. Then he turned to look at me.

"And now," he said, "will you be wise? Will you be guided? Will you let me take this glass away without another word? Or are you too curious for that? Think before you answer, for I'll do whatever you decide. You can either be left as you were before I came, none the wiser or richer. Or if you wish, you can experience a whole new world of knowledge that might lead to fame and power, while your mind will be challenged by something that would stagger the Devil himself."

"Sir," I said, trying to sound a lot calmer than I felt, "you're talking in riddles, and I'm not sure I believe a word you say. But I've come too far tonight to stop before I reach the end."

"Very well," replied my visitor. "But remember you're a doctor, Lanyon. What I'm about to show you must remain our professional secret. And now you, who have been narrow minded, who have denied spiritual medicine, who have mocked your superiors – behold!"

He put the glass to his lips and downed the contents in a single gulp. He cried, then reeled and staggered, clutching the table for support. He stared at me with fixed eyes and gasped with an open mouth.

As I looked, he seemed to change. His whole body swelled, his face became suddenly black, and the features melted and altered. The next moment I jumped to my feet and pressed my back against the wall, my arm raised to shield myself from what I'd seen, my mind filled with terror.

"Oh no!" I screamed, again and again. For there before my eyes, pale and shaken, half fainting, half groping in front of him, like a man returned from the dead, stood – Henry Jekyll!

What he told me over the next hour, I cannot bring myself to write down. I saw what I saw, I heard what I heard, and my soul sickened at it. Yet now that the sight has faded from my eyes, I begin to ask myself if I still believe it, and I can't answer.

My life has been shaken to its roots. I can't sleep; the deadliest of terrors is with me, all hours of the day and night. I feel that my days are numbered and that I'm going to die. And yet I shall die in disbelief.

I can't think about the sorry tale of shame that Jekyll told, admittedly through tears of regret, without a start of horror. I will just say this Utterson, and, if you can bring yourself to believe it, it will be more than enough.

The creature who had crept into my house that night was, as Jekyll himself confessed, the foul murderer hunted in every corner of the land – Edward Hyde.

H. LANYON.

Chapter 13

An experiment in evil

The confession of Dr. Henry Jekyll – Part I

I was born into a wealthy family. I grew up to become a hard-working individual, keen to earn the respect of everyone I met. So you might have thought that a distinguished and successful future lay ahead of me.

But I also had a reckless streak.

Now I know that such a characteristic has been the source of happiness for many people, but it didn't fit easily with the serious and respectable character I wanted to present to the world.

So it was that I hid this other side of my personality away, even though it never left me completely.

I hope, Utterson, that you don't think I was being a hypocrite; because I firmly believe that I was as much myself when entertaining dangerous thoughts as I was when I was studying medicine.

In fact, it was my scientific studies that eventually led me to a possible solution to the problem I had in my life.

I came to realize that a man is not one thing, but two. I say two, because that's the number I've discovered. It may well be that future scientists will reveal many more characters within a single human being.

Even before I began my research into the subject, I'd had a dream that it might be possible to separate out an individual's personalities. It seemed to me that if the good side of a person could be housed in one identity and the bad side in another, it would prevent the good side feeling guilty and the bad side from feeling miserable. I felt it was a curse that the good and bad should be tied together, struggling against each other.

But how could they be separated?

My chemical experiments led me to believe that the human body was capable of change. I won't go into detail about the exact nature of my findings for two reasons. Firstly, because I've since learned to my cost that the mixture of our different characteristics is something which we human beings must endure, and only disaster follows if you attempt to fight nature; secondly, because my discoveries were ultimately incomplete, as my story all too painfully shows.

Suffice to say that I managed to create a drug that could reduce the levels of the respectable side of a personality and raise the levels of the darker side.

I hesitated for a long time before I tested my theory, for I knew that I risked death. Any drug that could control the very identity of a human being was also capable of destroying that person. But the temptation of such a unique and groundbreaking discovery soon overcame any fears I might have had.

It took some years to perfect the basic solution. From my experiments I knew that the last ingredient required was a particular salt. As such, I'd bought a large quantity of this substance from a wholesale chemist.

And so, late one fateful night, I added the salt to the solution, watched them boil and smoke together in the glass and, when the bubbling had subsided, summoned up all my courage and drank the potion.

There followed the most searing pains, a grinding of my bones, a terrible sickness and a feeling of depression so great it might surely be worse than death itself. Then the agony subsided and I suddenly felt much better.

This new sensation was strange. I felt younger,

lighter and fitter. From the first breath of this, my
new life, I also realized that I was ten times more
wicked than my old self, and the thought
delighted me. It was only when I stretched out my
hands in pleasure at my transformation that I was
suddenly aware I'd become physically smaller.

There was no mirror in my study at that time
and I was desperate to view my new self. This
meant crossing over to the house. Although it was
still dark outside, it would soon be light.
However, I knew the servants would all still be
asleep. So, filled with a feeling of hope, I decided
to venture as far as my bedroom.

I crossed the yard and crept through the
corridors, a stranger in my own house, until I
finally reached my room. There it was that I first
set eyes on Edward Hyde.

I can only offer a theory as to why my new self
was so much smaller than my previous one. I
believe that because the evil side of my nature had
been repressed for so long, it was much less

developed than the good side, which had been predominantly on show. So it was, I think, that Edward Hyde was so much slighter and younger than Henry Jekyll.

Evil too was written upon this new face, and it had left me looking somehow deformed. Yet when I looked at that ugly profile in the mirror, I didn't feel repelled. Instead I was glad to see it. This man was me as well. It seemed only natural and human. If anything, to me Hyde was more lively and uncomplicated than the dull and imperfect Jekyll.

I was later to discover that no one could come near Edward Hyde without being disturbed by his appearance. I think this is because all human beings we meet are composed of good and evil, whereas Edward Hyde was unique in being evil alone.

I paused for a moment in front of the mirror. The second part of the experiment had yet to be attempted. It remained to be seen if I'd lost my former identity forever and would therefore have no option but to flee from a house that was no longer mine.

So I hurried back to my study and prepared the solution as before. Once more, I suffered the terrible pains of physical and mental change. But I was soon returned to the character and form of Henry Jekyll.

That night was a fatal turning point. If I'd taken a more generous view of matters, I could have shared the results of my experiment with the world. But the selfish side of my personality had gained a foothold, and I'd already begun to tire of Henry Jekyll's dull, serious life. I was a well-known and respected scientist, but I was growing old, and the dryness of my world of study was losing its appeal. From the more lurid reports of newspapers and other publications, I was aware of a world of almost animalistic thrills that existed elewhere in society. Many times in the past I'd wanted to experience that life, but my good nature had always held me back. The only way to end my constant frustration was to stop that goodness from having any say in the matter.

So it was that my new power tempted me until I could resist no more. For I only had to take a sip of the solution to throw off the body of the noted professor and take on that of Edward Hyde.

Chapter 14

A double life

The confession of Dr. Henry Jekyll – Part II

I made practical preparations for my twin existence. I rented a furnished house in Soho (to which Hyde was later tracked by the police) and engaged a housekeeper whom I knew I could persuade to keep quiet about Hyde's comings and goings.

Meanwhile, at my other home in the square, I told my servants that Mr. Hyde was to have the run of the house. I made several visits there in my alternate guise, so Poole and the others might become familiar with Hyde.

Next I drew up that Will that you objected to so much, Utterson. This meant that if I wanted to stop being Dr. Jekyll for whatever reason, I could take on the form of Edward Hyde without suffering any financial loss.

With all these safeguards in place, I began to profit from the immunity of my double life. In the past, men have hired thugs to conduct crimes for them, to give themselves an alibi. But I was the first person to walk the streets with his head held high one moment, and the next, to strip off this shell of respectability and step into another world as someone else. Think of it – I didn't even exist! I only had to escape back to my laboratory, swallow the draught that I always had standing ready, and whatever terrible things Edward Hyde had done, he would disappear. There in his place, sitting quietly at home, would be a man who was above suspicion – Dr. Henry Jekyll.

The pleasures that I enjoyed while in disguise were at first merely undignified. But in the hands of Edward Hyde, they gradually became more monstrous. The character I'd set free from my body was wicked and villainous. He thought of no one but himself. Everything he did was for his own satisfaction.

I – that is Henry Jekyll – was sometimes appalled by what Edward Hyde had done. But the situation was so unusual that it made it hard to feel remorse about what he was doing. It was Hyde, and Hyde alone, who was guilty after all. Jekyll was unchanged, and was seemingly as good a man as ever. I would even try to undo the evil done by Hyde wherever possible. And so I convinced myself that my conscience was clear.

I have no desire to go into the details of the terrible acts that I committed. I just want to point out the ways in which they were not without dangers; dangers which would eventually lead to my downfall.

On one occasion, my act of cruelty to a child roused the anger of her family and several others, to the extent that there were moments when I feared for my life. In order to save his own skin, Edward Hyde was forced to pay the child's father with a cheque from the account of Henry Jekyll.

To prevent this from happening again, I opened an account at another bank under the name of Edward Hyde. By disguising my own handwriting I was able to supply my double with a signature. I'd had a narrow escape, but I believed I was safe from discovery once more.

Two months before the murder of Sir Danvers Carew, I returned late at night from one of my adventures. When I woke the next morning I experienced the oddest sensation. I knew that I was in my bedroom in the house in the square. But as I tried to make out the furniture around me, my mind kept throwing up visions of the little room in Soho where I spent the nights as Hyde. I was wondering why, when I noticed my hand.

Henry Jekyll's hand was large, firm and pale pink in hue. But the hand I was looking at now was dusky and thin, shaded with a thick growth of hair. It was the hand of Edward Hyde.

I lay staring at it for some time before the full, terrible meaning of what had happened struck me. I scrambled out of bed and dashed to the mirror. My blood ran cold at the sight that met my eyes. I'd gone to bed as Henry Jekyll, but I'd woken as Edward Hyde.

How had this happened, I asked myself? And what could I do to reverse it?

All my drugs were in my study. That would mean a long journey down two flights of stairs, through the back passage, across the open courtyard and through the laboratory. I knew that the servants would be up and about and bound to notice me. Then, with relief, I remembered that they were already used to seeing me coming and going as my other self.

I quickly dressed as well as I was able to in

clothes too large for me, and passed through the house. Poole was shocked to see Hyde at that time of day, but ten minutes later Dr. Jekyll was sitting down to breakfast.

Alas I had little appetite. This incident seemed to suggest that some kind of final reckoning was imminent and I began to think more seriously about the dangers of my double existence.

In the past, the drug had not always produced an immediate transformation into Hyde, and I'd been forced sometimes to double or even triple the dose. As a result, it had seemed to me lately that Edward Hyde had grown slightly in height and become rather stronger. In the light of this morning's accident, I began to wonder if I had gone from a position of not being able to free myself from Jekyll, to one where I might be trapped within the form of Hyde.

I had to choose between the two. I weighed up the pros and cons of being each man.

Jekyll shared in the pleasures and adventures of

Hyde. But Hyde never thought about Jekyll. As far as he was concerned, the doctor was just a method of escape from his crimes.

To remain as Jekyll would mean I'd be starved of the wild life I'd recently come to enjoy. But if I remained as Hyde, I would be saying farewell to a world of learning and socializing and would be despised and friendless forever.

Jekyll would mourn the departure of his other life. Hyde wouldn't even care what he'd lost.

I chose the life of a good man in the end, though it turned out I didn't have the strength to stick to it. At that moment however, I was happy to remain the elderly, discontented doctor, surrounded by his friends with dreams of an honest future. So I said goodbye to the youth and secret pleasures that I'd enjoyed in the disguise of Hyde.

I must have had some unconscious doubts about my decision though, as I decided to keep the rooms in Soho and to store Hyde's clothes in my study. However, for two months I was true to my word. In fact I led a life that was even more respectable than before, which helped to ease my guilt.

But, as time went on, respectability began to lose its appeal and my mind started to hark back towards the excitement I'd enjoyed as Hyde.

At last, in a moment of weakness, I could stand it no more. I ran to my study, made up that fateful solution and swallowed the transforming mixture.

Chapter 15

The final battle

The confession of Dr. Henry Jekyll – Part III

My devil had been caged for a long time, and he came out roaring. Even as I sipped the potion, I was aware of a wilder, angrier feeling coming over me than had ever been the case before.

It must have been this insane anger that led to my impatience with poor Sir Danvers Carew. Only a madman could have acted as I did on that night. I had chosen to throw away that basic decency which stops even the worst of us from turning into animals.

As I attacked my victim, I took delight in every blow. It was only when I ran out of energy that I suddenly felt a cold chill of terror at what I'd done. For I realized my own life was now at risk from the forces of the law.

I fled from the scene of my crime with a mixture of excitement and fear. My appetite for evil had been satisfied, but my appetite for life was now under threat.

Rushing to the house in Soho, I quickly destroyed any papers which might incriminate me. Then I set off through the lamplit streets, gloating over my crime, while listening out for the footsteps of anyone who might try to catch me.

When I reached the safety of the study above the laboratory, there was a smile on my lips as I drank down the potion. But the transformation had barely finished before Henry Jekyll fell to his knees to pray to God for forgiveness.

As the horrible visions of what had occurred that night swam before my eyes, I decided then and there that my life of self-indulgence was over. As I made the decision, I felt a kind of joy. The terrible crime that had been committed that night meant that it was impossible for Hyde ever to exist again. Whether I liked it or not, I was now confined to my good self. I locked the door that led to the side street and ground the key under my heel.

The next day came the news that someone had witnessed Edward Hyde murder Sir Danvers Carew, M.P. I was glad that this tragic incident had been made public. Jekyll was now my place of refuge. If Hyde peered out for an instant, he would be arrested and executed for his crime.

I decided that I would make up for my past. As such, I spent the final months of last year working on new medicines that would relieve the suffering of the sick. The days passed quietly, almost happily.

I enjoyed my new life at first, but as time went on, the bad side of me, so long chained up, growled to be set free. Not that I dreamed of bringing Hyde back to life – that idea was too frightening to consider. No, it was as Henry Jekyll that I was once more tempted to the dark side of life. And yet I wasn't alarmed. This fall back into my old ways seemed natural. It was a return to the days before I'd made my discovery.

The final chapter in my sorry saga began on a fine January day as I was sitting on a bench in Regent's Park. The animal within me was coming to the surface, fuelled by the memories of my past sins. But unlike those around me, my good deeds would more than make up for whatever bad things I did. Or so I told myself.

At that very moment, a horrid sickness came over me, coupled with a terrible shuddering. As these sensations passed away, I suddenly felt bolder and braver, with a disregard for danger. I looked down. My clothes hung baggily on my shrunken limbs. The hand that lay on my knee was dark and hairy. I was Edward Hyde again. A moment before, I had been safe and respected. Now I was a homeless, hunted man – a known murderer fit only for the hangman's noose.

I'd noticed on previous occasions that in my second guise I was bolder and more cunning. As Henry Jekyll, I might have panicked at this moment, but as Hyde I rose to the challenge.

My drugs were in my study. But how was I to reach them? I'd sealed the side street door. If I entered by the house, my own servants would surely hand Hyde over to the police. I needed help, and I thought of Lanyon. But even if I could make my way across London to his home without being apprehended, how was I, a total stranger to his eyes, to persuade him to search the study of his old friend Henry Jekyll? Then I remembered that Hyde and Jekyll had one thing in common – my handwriting. I conceived a plan and set about putting it into operation.

I adjusted my clothes as best I could, hailed a passing cab and drove to a hotel in Portland Street. The driver smirked at the sight of my baggy clothes, but I gnashed my teeth at him in devilish fury and his smile soon vanished. As I entered the hotel, the black expression on my face made the receptionist tremble. He took my orders obediently, leading me to a private room before bringing me writing materials.

Hyde was in danger of his life now, and this brought out new feelings of anger and violence. Yet this creature I'd become kept his fury under control, and I composed two letters: one to Lanyon, the other to Poole. I ordered them to be posted and spent all day by the fire in my room, biting my nails. I dined alone, then when it was dark, I set off in a cab, driving to and fro across the city. Nothing lived in me now but fear and hatred. When I thought the driver had begun to be suspicious, I dismissed him and carried on on foot. I walked fast, haunted by my fears, muttering to myself, skulking through the back streets and counting the minutes until midnight.

When I reached Lanyon's house, the look of fear on my old friend's face made me feel more like my other self. A change had come upon me. It was no longer a fear of being executed that frightened me, but the horror of being Hyde. Lanyon had done as I'd instructed, and in a few moments I was Henry Jekyll once again. I was in a kind of daze as Lanyon went into a rage about what I'd done, and I was still in that daze when I arrived home and went to bed. I slept deeply after the long day I'd just experienced.

I woke the next morning shaken, weakened, but refreshed. I still hated and feared the thought of the brute that slept inside me, and I hadn't forgotten the appalling dangers of the day before. But I was home once more, close to my chemicals, and hugely relieved to have escaped.

I was strolling around the courtyard after breakfast when I suddenly felt the terrible change begin to come over me again. I just had time to reach the seclusion of my study before I was once more raging with the passions of Hyde. It took a double dose of my potion to return me to my other self. But six hours later, the change occurred again and I went through the same ritual. From that day onwards, I found it harder and harder to remain as Jekyll for any length of time. At all hours of the day or night, the change came over me. If I slept, or even dozed off in my chair for a moment, I always awoke as Hyde. Under the strain of this impending doom and the sleeplessness that went with it, I became feverish and weak. I could only think of one thing, the horror of my other self. When I slept, my dreams were filled with images of terror. The powers of Hyde seemed to have grown with the sickliness of Jekyll. It was only the fear of execution that made Hyde keep returning to his better self. He loathed Jekyll, and he defaced my books, burned my letters and destroyed a portrait of my father. Despite all this,

I can still find it in my heart to pity him.

My punishment might have gone on for years, were it not for the misfortune that has now occurred and which has finally cut me off from my own body and personality.

My supply of salt, which I'd never renewed since the first experiment, began to run low, so I sent out for a fresh supply. I mixed it with the other ingredients as before, but when I drank it, nothing happened. You'll learn from Poole how I'd had London searched for a replacement, without success. I now believe that that very first supply of salt was impure in some unknown way, and it was that impurity which caused my potion to work.

About a week has passed, and I'm writing this statement under the influence of the last of the old powders. This is the last time then, short of a miracle, that Henry Jekyll can think his own thoughts or see his own face in the mirror. I mustn't wait any longer to bring my writing to an end. It's only by a mixture of caution and good luck that this document has so far escaped destruction. If the transformation should occur while I'm writing, Hyde will tear this statement to pieces. But if I can finish it well before the next change, then Hyde will probably be too self-absorbed to destroy it. In any case, the doom that is closing in on us both has already crushed him. I know that when the next transformation occurs, Hyde will sit shuddering and weeping in this chair, or else pace up and down, listening out for the sound of his pursuers.

Will Hyde be caught and hung? Or will he find the courage to escape that fate at the last moment. Who knows? I'm past caring. This is my true moment of death and what happens next concerns someone else. Here then, as I put down my pen and seal up my confession, I bring the life of unhappy Henry Jekyll to an end.

THE END

Robert Louis Stevenson

Robert Lewis Balfour Stevenson was born in Edinburgh, Scotland on 13th November 1850. His father, Thomas, was a lighthouse engineer, as were his grandfather and two of his uncles.

Robert Stevenson was a sickly child and often suffered from coughs and fevers. As such, he spent a lot of time away from school and was taught at home by private tutors.

His passion for storytelling began at a young age and he would often recite tales to his parents. He soon began writing his stories down, encouraged by his father. When Stevenson was sixteen, his father paid for the printing of his son's first book – an account of the 1666 rebellion of the Scottish Covenanters (a group opposed to the interference of kings in the affairs of the Church).

In 1867, Stevenson went to Edinburgh University to study engineering, although he had no real interest in the subject and avoided lectures whenever he could. During the holidays, he would travel around Scotland with his father to visit the family's engineering works and various lighthouses.

In 1868, Stevenson changed the spelling of his middle name to 'Louis' and informed his father that he wanted to become a professional writer. His parents accepted this, although, to provide something to fall back on, it was agreed that he should read Law at Edinburgh. Around this time, he also joined the LJR (Liberty, Justice, Reverence) Club, much to the annoyance of his parents, as it encouraged its members to disregard everything they had been taught.

Following trips to one of his cousins in England, Stevenson became friends with many of the writers working in London at that time, including Leslie Stephen, a magazine editor. On a visit to Edinburgh, Stephen introduced Stevenson to William Henley, a lively character with a wooden leg, believed by many to be the inspiration for Long John Silver in Stevenson's 1883 novel *Treasure Island*.

In 1873, Stevenson went to the French Riviera to recover from another bout of ill health. It was the first of many trips, and he would go on to spend time with the many artists' groups near Paris.

At the age of twenty-four, he qualified as a solicitor, although he never went into the profession, concentrating instead on his career as a writer.

During a trip to France in 1876, he met and fell in love with Fanny Osbourne, an American mother of three. When Fanny returned to California in 1878, Stevenson set off to join her, although the long journey had a bad effect on his health. He married Fanny in 1880 and the pair returned to Britain along with Fanny's son, Lloyd.

In an attempt to find somewhere to live that would improve his physical condition, Stevenson spent the next seven years in different locations across Britain and France. It was while he was staying in Bournemouth, Dorset, in 1885 that he wrote *The Strange Case of Dr. Jekyll and Mr. Hyde*. Stevenson later said that the ideas for several of the scenes in the novel came to him in a dream. According to his wife, she was woken by cries of horror from her husband in the small hours of the morning. Assuming he was having a terrible nightmare, she woke him up, only for Stevenson to reply angrily, "Why did you wake me? I was dreaming a fine bogey tale."

After Stevenson had written the story, he showed it to Fanny for her comments. When she was critical of the style he'd used, he began again, completing the tale in six days. Legend has it that he burned the original manuscript to avoid the temptation of returning to it.

Despite his poor health, it was during this period that Stevenson wrote some of his most famous and popular books. Alongside *Dr. Jekyll and Mr. Hyde*, there were *Treasure Island, Kidnapped* and *The Black Arrow*.

After the death of his father in 1887, Stevenson followed his doctor's advice and set off with his wife, stepson and mother for a change of climate.

They were heading for Colorado, USA, but when they arrived in New York, they decided to spend the winter there instead. It was there that Stevenson began work on a historical adventure novel, *The Master of Ballantrae*.

In the summer of 1888, Stevenson and his family chartered a yacht and began a tour of the eastern and central Pacific. Among other places, they visited the Hawaiian Islands, Tahiti, New Zealand and the Samoan Islands. Along the way, he finished *The Master of Ballantrae* and also wrote *The Bottle Imp*. His book *In the South Seas*, published after his death, was Stevenson's account of one of the cruises he went on during this period. A later voyage of 1890 was described by Fanny in her own book, *The Cruise of the Janet Nichol*. One of the passengers on this trip, island trader Jack Buckland, later became the inspiration for the character of Tommy Hadden in Stevenson's adventure novel *The Wrecker*, which he co-wrote with his stepson Lloyd.

In 1890 Stevenson bought a piece of land on the Samoan island of Uplou and set up home in the village of Vailma. He involved himself in the lives of the locals and often defended them against the bad management of the European officials who ruled over them. He became so integrated with the islanders that he called himself *Tusitala* which means 'teller of tales' in Samoan.

For a time, Stevenson was worried that his ill health would return. He also grew concerned about the quality of his work. But these feelings eventually passed and, among other books, he went on to write *Weir of Hermiston*, which he considered to be the best thing he had ever written.

On 3rd December, 1894, Stevenson was struggling to open a bottle of wine when he collapsed and died within a few hours, probably from a stroke.

The Samoans buried their friend *Tusitala* on Mount Vaea in a spot overlooking the sea. The master storyteller's own tale was at an end.

A selection of books by
Robert Louis Stevenson

Treasure Island (1883)

Prince Otto (1885)

The Strange Case of Dr. Jekyll and Mr. Hyde (1886)

Kidnapped (1886)

The Merry Men and other Tales and Fables (1887)

The Black Arrow: A Tale of the Two Roses (1888)

The Master of Ballantrae (1889)

The Wrong Box (1889), co-written with Lloyd Osbourne

The Wrecker (1892), co-written with Lloyd Osbourne

Island Nights' Entertainments (1893), includes

The Bottle Imp short story, originally published in 1891

Catriona (1893), a sequel to *Kidnapped*

The Ebb-Tide (1894), co-written with Lloyd Osbourne

Published after Stevenson's death:

Weir of Hermiston (1896), unfinished

In the South Seas (1896)